Vera's New School

Vera Rosenberry

Henry Holt and Company

New York

It was October, and Vera's family had moved to a new town. Now Vera was the new girl in school. She was told she was in Room 4 and Miss Roberts was her teacher.

Vera walked into the classroom and sat down at an empty desk.

All the children were chattering and laughing.

A boy came in and said to her, "This is my seat."

Vera's face turned red. She stood up and let the boy sit down.

The bell rang, and everyone was seated, except Vera.
The teacher, a lady with bluish hair, said, "You must
be the new girl."

In a small voice, Vera answered, "Yes, I am Vera."

"Well, Vera," Miss Roberts said, "there are some empty desks in the fourth row, so please be seated."

Vera was happy to sit down at her own desk.

It was art day, and soon the art teacher came in. He handed out big sheets of paper. Then he asked the class to draw a picture of their favorite pet.

Vera took out her box of crayons. She was not sure what to draw because she didn't have a pet.

She thought about the baby duck her father had brought home last Easter. It had eaten some dry cement in the garage and died. Vera could draw the little duck, but that made her too sad.

So Vera decided to draw an elephant instead. She loved elephants, and drawing one made her happy.

The art teacher walked up and down the aisles, saying what nice dogs and kittens, parakeets and fish everyone was making.

When he came to Vera, he said, "Hi, I'm Mr. Furnace. You must be new here." Then he looked at Vera's picture. "What a fine elephant you have drawn!"

Mr. Furnace held up Vera's picture to show the class.

"Do you have an elephant at home?" Mr. Furnace asked with a friendly wink.

The children laughed, and Vera's face turned red again. She wished she had drawn a picture of a dog. But it was too late.

At recess, Vera walked out to the playground. Many children were playing games. Vera hoped someone would ask her to join in, but no one did.

Vera sat on a swing and swung as
high as she could. She missed her
best friend, Anand.

Later, seated at the end of a long table, Vera began to eat her egg salad sandwich. Two girls across from her pointed at her lunch and made a funny face.

The girls whispered to each other and laughed. Vera didn't feel hungry anymore. She wanted to go home, but the afternoon spread out endlessly before her.

After lunch, there was a special assembly outside on the school lawn. Jungle Larry was coming to teach the children about the wild animals he studied in Africa and Asia.

Miss Roberts told everyone to choose a partner.

All the children paired up, but there was no one for Vera.
She had to hold her teacher's hand at the front of the line.

Vera sat on a little rise so she could see better. Maybe
Jungle Larry would have an elephant, and he would
need someone to help him feed it.

Another girl from Vera's class sat down beside her.
Vera remembered her name was Lydia.

After a long introduction by the principal, Mr. Mounts, Jungle Larry leapt out of the back of a truck.

He swept off his big hat and smiled.
An enormous snake was wrapped
around his body. Everyone stared,
spellbound.

Vera and Lydia leaned forward to get a closer look.

A pungent smell filled the air.

Jungle Larry's voice was deep and loud and exciting.

As he spoke about his travels, he reached into his truck.

"This next animal," he explained, "had a badly injured foot when I found him. He can no longer manage in the wild, so he is my special companion now."

Just then Miss Roberts thrust her head between Lydia and Vera.

"GIRLS!" she whispered loudly, right in their ears. "You are covered, simply COVERED, with red ants! Get up right away!"

Vera and Lydia looked down. They had been sitting on
a big anthill. Ants were everywhere—inside their skirts
and blouses and even in their underpants. And the ants
were starting to bite!

The two girls ran into the school washroom and tore off all their clothes, wiping the red ants away as quickly as they could. Tiny welts broke out where the ants had bitten them.

The school nurse came in and dabbed soothing cream on all their bites. After a little while, Vera and Lydia put on their clothes and went back outside.

By this time, Jungle Larry was saying good-bye. Everyone was clapping.

Vera and Lydia stood on the lawn while teachers and children brushed past them, talking about the exciting show.

"We missed everything," Vera moaned. This had been a truly awful day.

"Pair up, please, class," said Miss Roberts. "Come along, girls."

Lydia took Vera's hand and smiled. "Let's be friends," she said.
"Will you be my partner?"

Vera looked at Lydia and nodded. She smiled, too.

The two new friends walked back to Room 4, chatting happily. Every now and then, they stopped to scratch a tender spot.

To the real Lydia,
who became my friend when I was the new girl in school

Henry Holt and Company, LLC
Publishers since 1866
175 Fifth Avenue
New York, New York 10010
www.henryholtchildrensbooks.com

Henry Holt® is a registered trademark of Henry Holt and Company, LLC.
Copyright © 2006 by Vera Rosenberry
All rights reserved.
Distributed in Canada by H. B. Fenn and Company Ltd.

Library of Congress Cataloging-in-Publication Data
Rosenberry, Vera.
Vera's new school / Vera Rosenberry.—1st ed.
p.   cm.
Summary: Everything seems to go wrong for Vera on her first day at a new school,
until a classmate shares one of her mishaps.
ISBN-13: 978-0-8050-7613-4 / ISBN-10: 0-8050-7613-1
[1. Schools—Fiction. 2. Friendship—Fiction.] I. Title.
PZ7.R719155Ven 2006   [E]—dc22   2005020052

First Edition—2006
The artist used watercolor on Lanaquarelle paper to create the illustrations for this book.
Printed in the United States of America on acid-free paper. ∞

1 3 5 7 9 10 8 6 4 2